LOOICE WALKS FOR PRESIDENT

piano/vocal

Book and Lyrics by Ben Goldstein
Music by Phillip Namanworth

LOOICE WALKS FOR PRESIDENT

Musical Numbers

(1) LOOICE
BIRDS: "YES WE SAW HIM TOO... HE WAS..."
A PENGUIN & BIRDS
BIRDS: "YES WE SAW HIM TOO... HE WAS..."

B
ANIMAL CRACKER DREAMS____ SELLING JELLY BEANS____ BUILDING
B♭   G7   E♭7
SNOWMEN IN THE SAND____ AS HE WRITES____ UPON THE SAND ____
G7   F7   A   F#7
L - O - O - I - C E THAT'S HIS NAME L - O - O - I - C - E THATS HIS NAME
B7   E♭   B7   E♭
C
DRAWING FACES ON BOARDS ____ PAINTING WALLS ON PICTURES AND WORDS
F

TRYING TO PUT OUT THE SUN ___ WITH HIS LEAKY WA-TER GUN YOU'LL NEVER DO IT.
A
B♭7
E♭7 +5
BIRD #1
BIRD #2
LOOIE   (I HOPE HE DOESN'T DO IT)   LOOIE   (IT'S THE
F♯
B♭7
A
E♭
B♭7
D   ALL
ONLY SUN WE'VE GOT)   TEACHING THE CLOUDS TO LAUGH ___   RE-CORDING HIS PHOTOGRAPH
E♭7
A
B♭7
E♭7
A
B♭7
PLANTING PEA-NUTS IN THE SAND ___   AS HE WRITES ___ UPON HIS
E♭7
A
B♭7
E♭7
A

NAND___ L-O-O-I-C-E THAT'S HIS NAME L-O-O-I-
FA7 B7 E7 B7
E
I-C-E
CUTTING OUT THE MOON ___ WIPING A WAY IT'S LAUGH
E7 F
(REVENGE IS BAD)
MAKING THE SUN GO DOWN ___ AS THE TIDE DISSAPEARS FROM THE
A B♭7
BIRD #3 PENGUIN PENGUIN
HO GROUND HE DREAM LOOIE___ NOW LOOIE YA COME DOWN FROM THE CEILING. LOOIE___ NOW LOOIE YOU COME
(L) NO!
E7+5 F# B7 A E7 B7

L. NO!
DOWN FROM THE CEILING   YOU OBVIOUSLY DON'T UNDERSTAND THE GRAVITY OF THE SITUATION.   LOUIE
E7
B7
E7
B

(2) THIS LITTLE GIRL

CHORUS
GROW
WHEN
B
CLOUDS HIDE THE SUN SHE MAKES DAY SEEM BRIGHTER
A
E7
WHEN YOU FEEL SAD SHE MAKES THINGS MUCH NICER
Asus A
VOICE
WHEN YOU'RE FEELING UP-SIDE DOWN SHE'S A RAINBOW HELPS YOU TURN YOUR HEAD A-

ROUND
A
B♭/A
A
C VOICE
VOICE
PEPPERMINT AND STAR-LIGHT MOON BEAMS AND DEW DROPS
A
B♭/F
F
CHORUS
PEPPERMINT AND STAR-LIGHT MOON BEAMS AND DEW DROPS
G
WITH THE TOUCH OF HER HAND THIS LITTLE GIRL COULD MAKE THE FLOWERS
B♭
C♯
B♭
D/E

GROW
Fin

(3) THE BOOGALOOIE

THE BOOGALOOS P.2
DANCED WITH AN ELEPHANT AND A LAW GARDO — HE HYPNOTIZED THE DEVIL DO THE BOO—GA LOO —
HYPNOTIZED THE DEVIL DO THE BOO—GA LOO — LET'S DANCE TOGE—THER — OH —
LOVE ONE ANO—THER — OH — HOLD HANDS TOGE—THER —
COME ON LOOIE DO IT TO US — COME ON LOO KE DO IT TO US —
-11-

LET'S DANCE TOGETHER ___ OH ___   LIVE ONE ANOTHER ___ OH ___
F   Eb   Bb   Ab
HOLD HANDS TOGETHER ___
F   Eb   Bb   C   Db
DON'T MATTER IF YOU'RE CATHOLIC OR BUDDHIST ___
D
ISLAMIC OR ATHEIST   HINDU OR JEWISH ___ BLACK WHITE OR YELLOW ___ PURPLE GREEN OR BLUE-ISH
E   F
EVERY ONE LOVES THE BOOGALOOLIE!
3X'S
Ab   A   D7

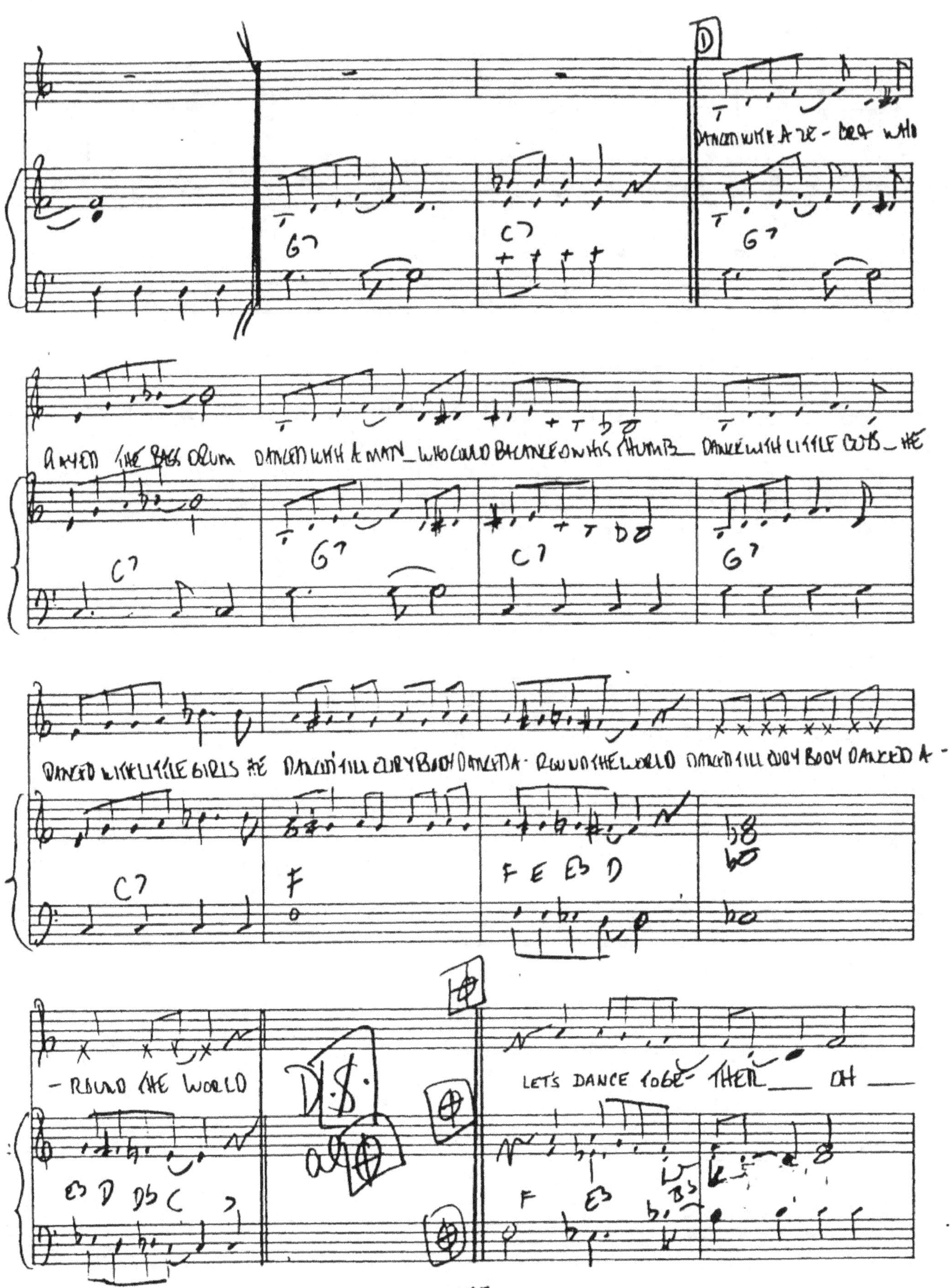
The Boogaloose P.t

D
Dancen with a ze-bra who
played the bass drum Dancen with a man_ who could balance on his thumb Dance with little cubs_ he
danced with little girls he danced till everybody danced a-round the world dancen till everybody danced a-
-round the world D.S. let's dance toge-ther__ oh__

G7 C7 G7
C7 G7 C7 G7
C7 F F E Eb D
Eb D Db C F Eb

-13-

DO THE BOOGA - LOO - ICE
Eb
Bb
Db
F
C7
F7
FINE

(4) LOOICE'S PRESIDENTIAL SPEECH

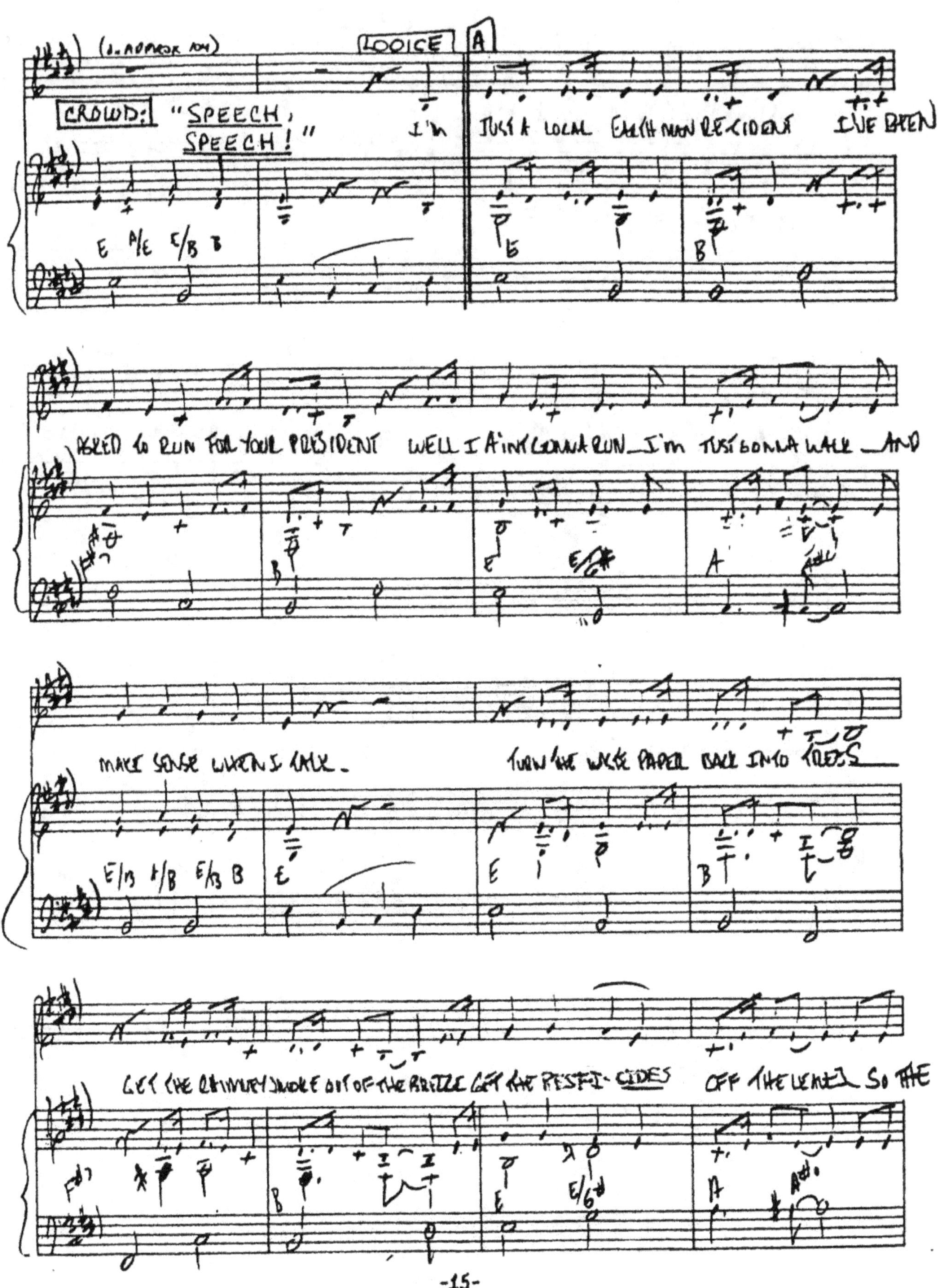

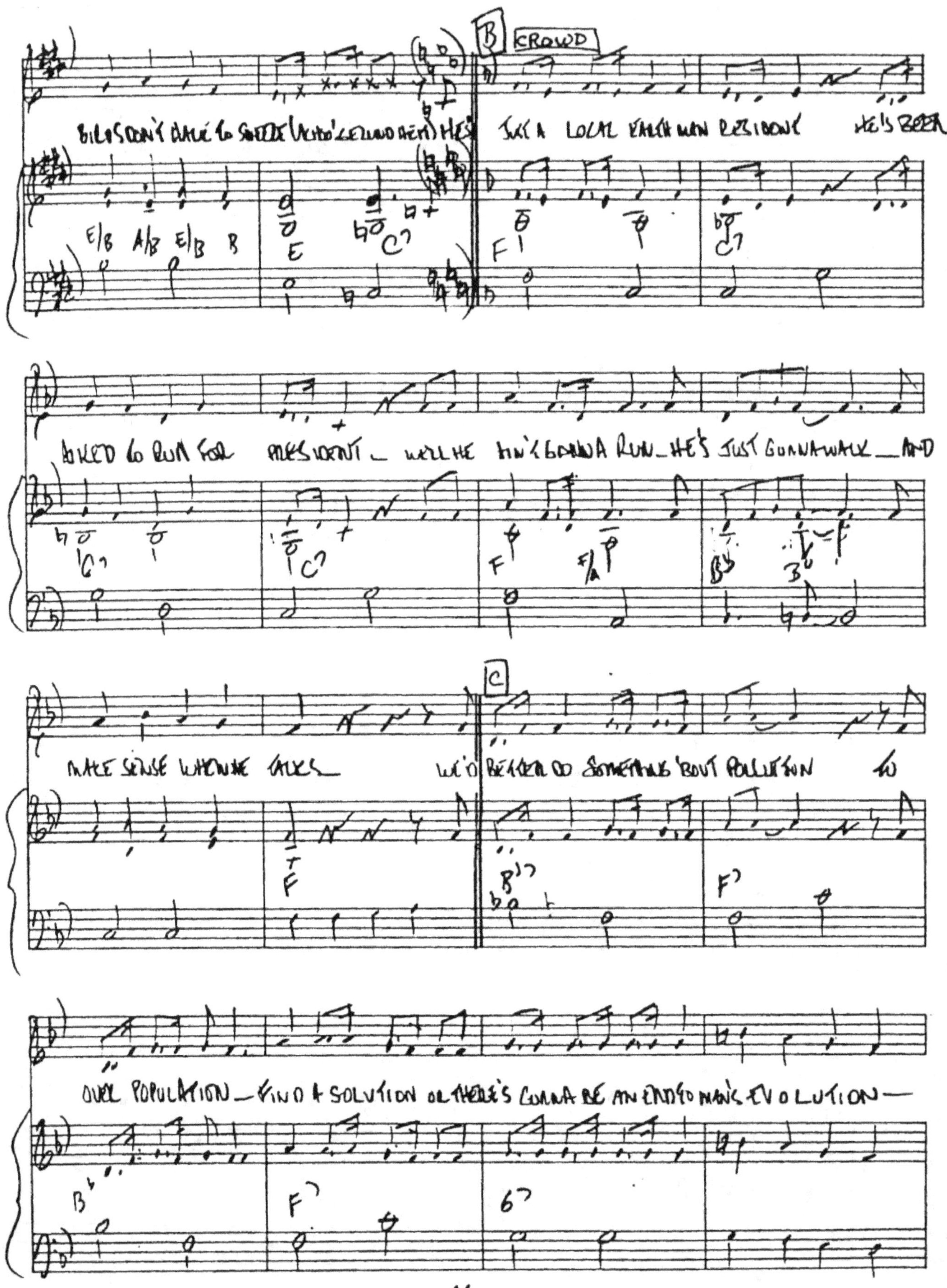
B
CROWD
BILLS DON'T CARE TO SPEAK (AND HE'S LAND AND) HE'S JUST A LOCAL EVERY MAN RESIDENT HE'S BEEN
E/B A/B E/B B
BORED TO RUN FOR PRESIDENT WELL HE AIN'T GONNA RUN HE'S JUST GONNA WALK AND
MAKE SENSE WHEN HE TALKS WE'D BETTER DO SOMETHING 'BOUT POLLUTION TO
C
OVER POPULATION FIND A SOLUTION OR THERE'S GONNA BE AN END TO MAN'S EVOLUTION

BOOLAH
(SOPRANOS) IT'S EXPECTED THIS YEAR 20 MILLION PEOPLE WILL DIE OF STARVATION.
CROWD
NOTHING TO EAT!
C7+5
B7
D
VOICE
WE COULD MAKE THE GREAT AS RUN WHERE IT'S DRY — MAKE THE DESERTS BLOOM — WET
E
B
UP TO THE SKY — FOOD FOR EVERY ONE IF WE TRY — MOTHER HOME LOOKIN' AND
B7
E7
A
APPLE PIE —
E CROWD
OH — MOTHER —
HOME

LOOKIN
KEEP ALL THE PEOPLE
MISTER HOME COOKIN AND
APPLE PIE
LOOKE F
I'm JUST A LOCAL EARTH MAN RESIDENT   I'VE BEE
ASKED TO RUN FOR PRESIDENT   WELL I AIN'T GONNA RUN   I'm JUST GONNA WALK   AND
MAKE SENSE WHEN I TALK
THANK YOU.
E/B A/B E/B A/B
A
E
A
FIN

(5) HOORAY TODAY

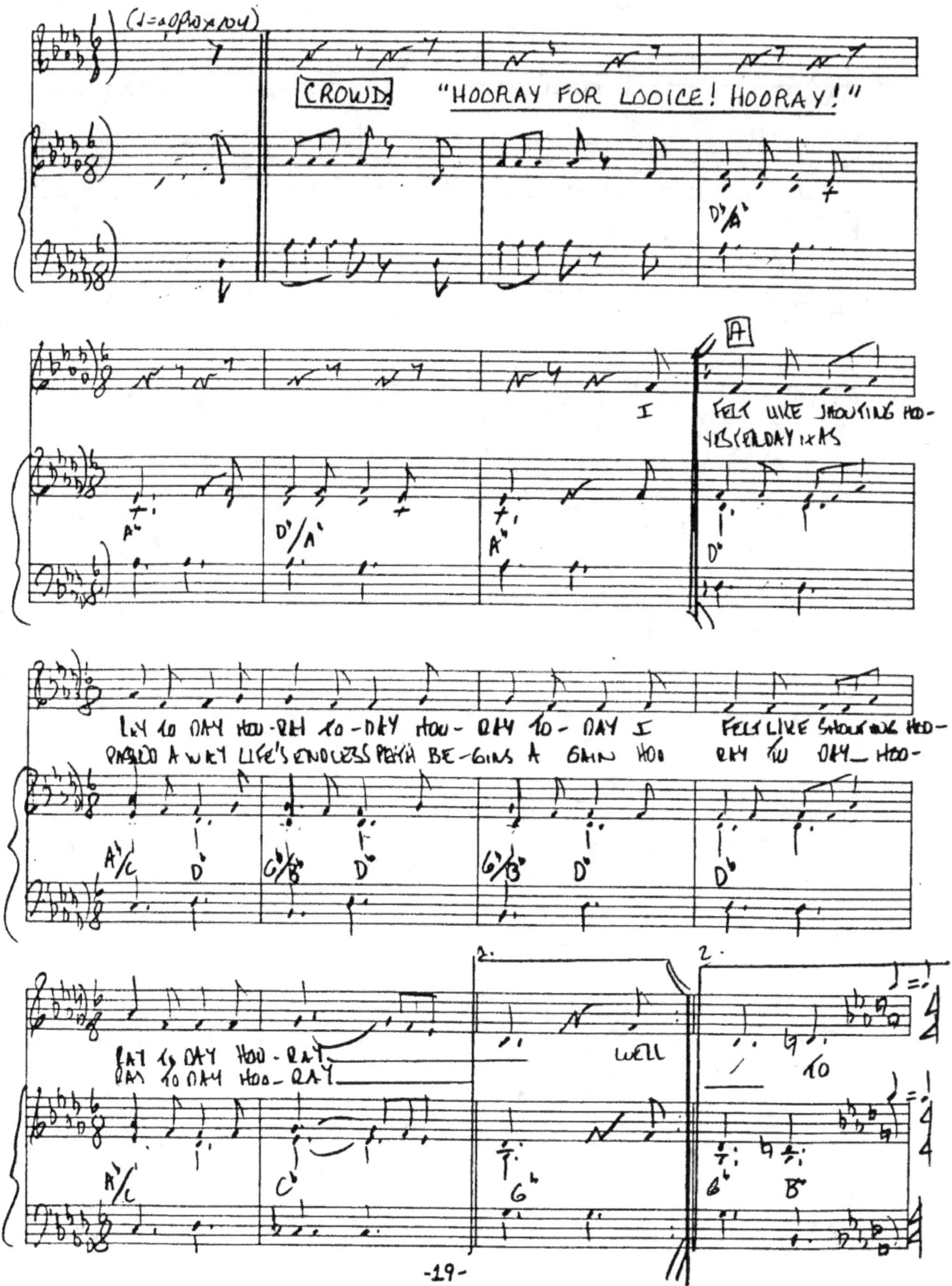

DAY   HOO-RAY TO-DAY   HOO-
RAY   HOO-RAY TO-DAY
CAREFREE IS THE WORLD SO GAY I   FEEL HIP HIP HIP   HIP TO DAY   THE
ON LET'S WALK COME ON LET'S PLAY   HOO-RAY TO DAY HOO   RAY TO DAY   COME

ONLY THING THERE IS TO SAY HOO-RAY
ON LET'S LAUGH COME ON LET'S RAY HOO-RAY
COME
TO-DAY HOO RAY TO-DAY
HOO-RAY HOO RAY TO DAY
WHAT DID YOU SAY? I SAID HOORAY WHAT DID YOU SAY I SAID HOORAY WHAT DID YOU SAY I SAID HOORAY TO

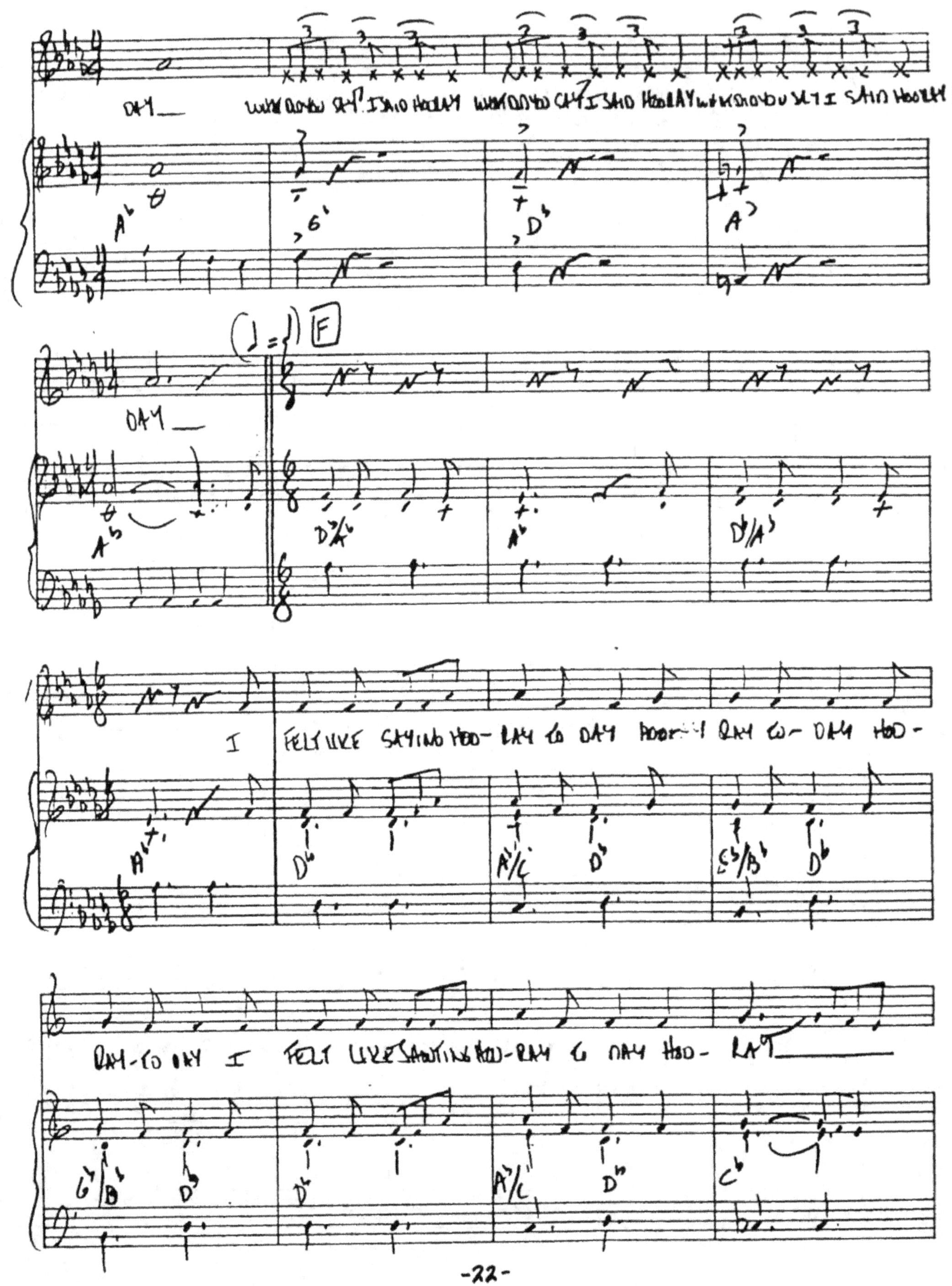
DAY
WHAT DID YOU SAY? I SAID HOORAY WHAT DID YOU SAY I SAID HOORAY WHAT DID YOU SAY I SAID HOORAY
DAY
I FELT LIKE SAYING HOO-RAY TO DAY HOORAY TO-DAY HOO-
RAY-TO DAY I FELT LIKE SAYING HOO-RAY TO DAY HOO-RAY

TO-DAY ___ HOO-RAY ___ TO-DAY ___ HOO-
RAY ___
HOO-RAY!

(6) MISTER SUNDAY

Mister Sunday 82
SUN - DAY   HELLO MISTER SUN - DAY
F- Eb/F   Bb   F- Eb/F   Asus9 A
I HAVE TO SMILE   WHEN SHE SAYS HI
D   Ab   Cb   D
SHE'S LIKE A RAINBOW   IN A SUNNY BLUE SKY
G   F   D/F#
CHORUS
CATCH THE MOON THE CHILD'S BALLOON DON'T LEAVE ME HERE A - LONE
Emi   B/D#   Cb   Bsus4 B
-25-

D
HEY MISTER SUNDAY
HEY MISTER SUNDAY
B
E/F#
B
E/F#
B
A/B
B
FIN

(7) CLAP YOUR HANDS

BRAINS COULD FALL OUT TRYIN TO UNDERSTAND _ WHO AM I? WHO AM I WHO I AM WHO I AM _
YOU COULD BE _ A ONE MAN BAND _ CLAP YOUR HANDS _
I
HEARD THAT A WOMAN HAD A BABY TODAY _ I HEARD THAT A MAN HAD PASSED AWAY _
WHAT CAN YOU DO _ ABOUT THE WORLD MOTHER'S WAYS _ BUT CLAP YOUR HANDS _
E
A/E
E
A/E
E
A/E
E
B
E
B
B
B
E
6
A

CLAP YOUR HANDS P.3
D
CLAP YOUR HANDS
GET IT ON GET IT ON
F# A B
T E
Jump and shout what it is what it is with it is all about work it out but work it out
A/E
E
A/E
E
work it on out CLAP YOUR HANDS
E
A/E
E
F
Bb/F
1.
2.
F
CLAP YOUR HANDS CLAP YOUR HANDS it's on
F
Bb/F
Bb/F
F

CLAP YOUR HANDS P.4
OLD CHILDREN'S RHYME THEY MUST HAVE KNOWN SOMETHING GOOD AT THE TIME YOU DON'T NEED NO MONEY CO
Bb/F   F   Bb/F   F
LAUGHTER TO DANCE ALL YOU GOTTA DO IS CLAP YOUR HANDS CLAP YOUR HANDS
Bb/F   F7+5   F   F
G
CLAP YOUR HANDS   CLAP YOUR HANDS
Bb/F   F   Bb/F   F
CLAP YOUR HANDS   YEAH!
Bb/F   F   Bb/F   F7
-30-   FIN

(8) Been Dere

B♭7
E♭7
B♭7
E♭7
B♭7
E♭7
A♭7
F♯7
D.C.
vamp til cutoff
B♭7
E♭7
BEFORE LOOICE SAYS: "AND YOU NOTICE YOUR FOOTPRINTS IS FACING THE OTHER WAY"

(8A) BEEN DERE (Reprise.)

(9) LOOICE IN THE STARGARDEN

ASTRONAUTS PASSING ON THEIR WAY TO THE MOON THEN
ONE DAY SANTA CLAUS MIS-PLACED ALL HIS TOYS
UNDERSCORE!

STARLIGHT P.3
PENGUIN & CHORUS
LAST
CUE "PRESENT OR TWO"
VOICE
HE GOT
CHROMIUM BALLELUM. ONYX ALUMINIUM —
F?
C?
T
F?
RUBIES SAPPHIRES GARLANDS SPARE TIRES BEAMS OF LIGHT AND SATELLITES
MIXED THE DAYLIGHT WITH THE NIGHT. TOOK THE DARKNESS FROM THE LIGHT
B♭7
E♭
C?
F?
MADE AN AMUSEMENT PARK. WHAT WAS OUT OF SIGHT HE GOT TOYS TOYS ON THE ASSEMBLY LINE. BIG TOYS LITTLE TOYS MORE + MORE
B♭7
E♭7
C?
E♭7
SANTA
SLOW:
LOOICE
SANTA LOOKED + SAID "HEY LOOICE" WHO ARE ALL THESE
FOR ____
FOR THE
SLOW!
E♭7
F-
B♭7/6
E♭7/6
E♭

D
CHILDREN OF JUPITER TOYS SU-PER JUPITER
TEN FEET AND HIGHER THAT GLITTER AND GLOW
VOICE
TOYS THAT SPIN AND TOYS THAT TURN THEY MAKE YOU LAUGH WHILE THEY MAKE YOU LEARN A
RAINBOW RIDE FROM U-RANUS TO THE RINGS OF SA-TURN

PENGUIN & CHORUS
E
HE MADE ANIMAL BEAST PENGUIN ZOOS FOR THE KIDS ANIMALS PLUS ZOO ANIMAL MAGIC MONTANA WHOS
LOUICE
PENGUIN
F
SANTA
THIS IS WHAT I DID SAID LOUICE. THE WAY NO THOUGHT OF GRAVITY
HE'S FREE AS HE CAN BE. A CHILD OF THE UNIVERSE
PENGUIN
CHILD LIKE YOU AND ME HE MADE A UNIVERSAL CIRCUS ZOO FOR THE

PENGUIN & CHORUS
KIDS WHO LIVE ON MERCURE AND FOR EARTH HE FOUND SANTA'S TOYS ON THE
RIT
DARK SIDE OF THE MOON
G♭ P
D♭ A♭/C B♭mi   A♭
E♭
Fin

(9A) LOOICE'S PRESIDENTIAL SPEECH (Reprise)

COOKIN'
FEED ALL THE PEO-PLE
A
E
A
MOTHER, HOME COOKIN' AND APPLE PIE
E/B A/B E/B A/B E/B B E

(10) ONE FAMILY
(♩ = approx 160) (MAJESTIC)
DEVIL: "...WHAT ABOUT IT, PENGUIN?"
PENGUIN & CROWD
THROUGH ALL WORLDS OF HEAVEN ___ AND THROUGH ALL WORLDS OF HELL ___
EACH THING WAS CRE-ATED ___ to USE THE OTHER WELL ___ BE-

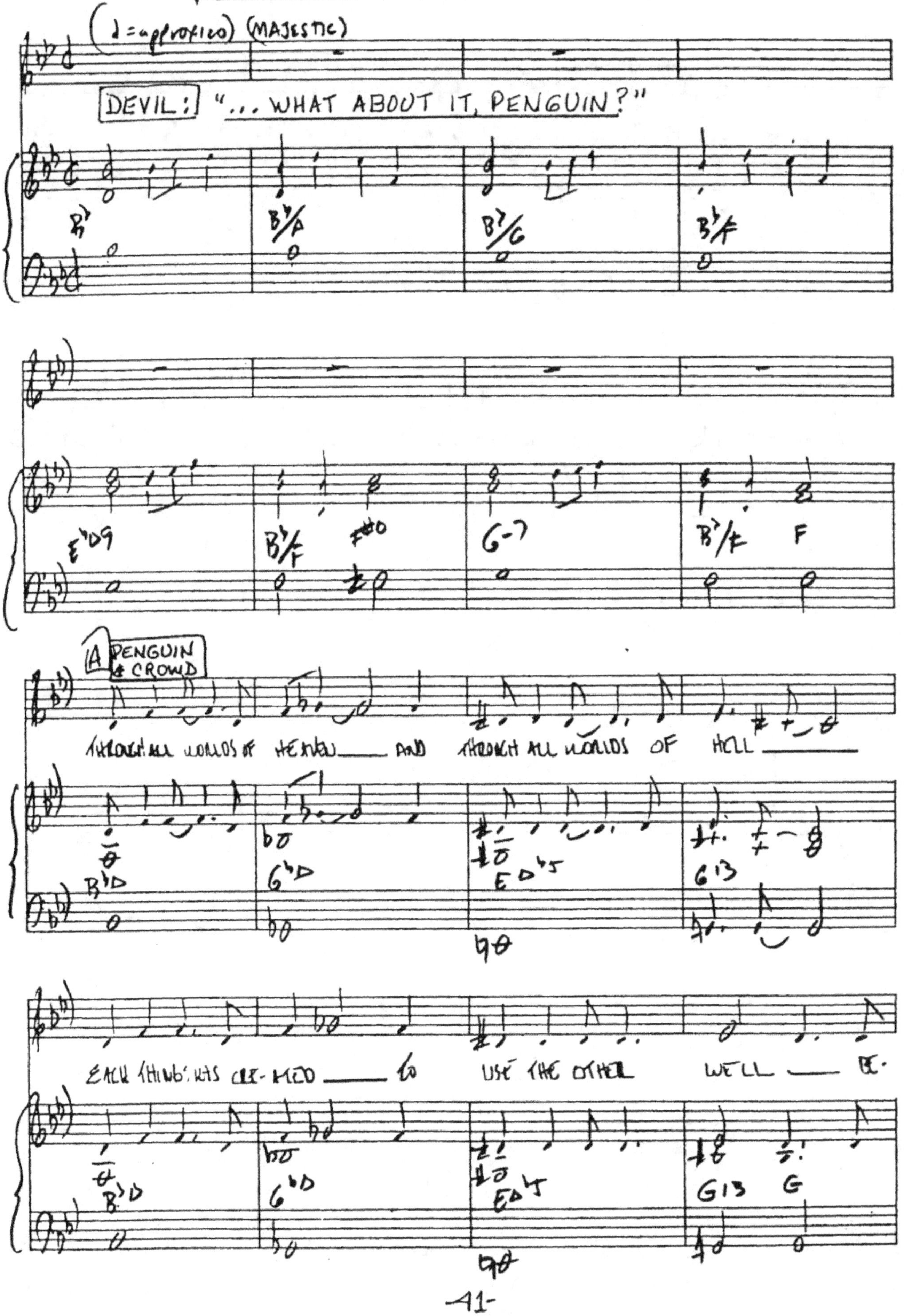

GINNING IN THE CLEAR SKY____ BE GINNING ON __ THE BLANK PAGE __ THE
6SUS4/A
G
G/F#
C/E
RICH MAN AND _ THE BEGGAR __ THE SINNER + THE SAGE __ ALL ARE ONE DIFFERENTLY
FSUS4
F
Bb
SAME AS YOU __ SAME AS ME ___ AND WE CAN ALL BE
Bb/A
Bb/G
Bb/F
G/A
FREE BECAUSE WE ARE   ONE   FAMILY___   ONE
D
A-7

FAMILY
LOVE FLOWS IN THE RIVERS
RIVERS FLOW INTO THE
SEA
THEY ALL COME TO-GETHER
JUST LIKE YOU
ME FLOW IN TO
ONE FAMILY
ONE FAMILY
(inst)

FEEL SO HAPPY IN-SIDE ______ LIFE IS A BEAUTIFUL
CHILD ______ FEEL SO HAPPY IN-SIDE ______ LIFE IS A BEAUTIFUL
CHILD IS A BEAUTIFUL LIFE IS A BEAUTIFUL CHILD ______

THE EARTH FEEDS US
C6b9
Eb6b5
G13
Bb9
G13 6
C6b9add/A
ALL THE EARTH CAN WELL AFFORD TO LOVE
C/F#
C/E
FSUS4
US ALL YOU AND ME LOVE US ALL YOU AND
Bb
Bb/A
Bb/G

J
me___ AND WE CAN ALL BE FREE BECAUSE WE ARE
ONE
K
FAMILY___ ONE FAMILY___ ONE___
L
FAMILY___ ONE FAMILY___

ONE ___ FAM - I -
B♭
emi
E♭/B♭
B♭
LU ___ .
E♭
FIN

(11) BOWS (BOOGALOOICE - ONE FAMILY)

THEN DO THE BOOGA LOO-IE
THE EARTH FEEDS US ALL THE
EARTH CAN WELL AFFORD TO LOVE US
ALL YOU AND ME LOVE US ALL YOU AND ME AND

WE CAN ALL BE FREE BECAUSE WE ARE ONE FAMILY
ONE FAMILY
ONE FAMILY
ONE FAMILY

ONE ____ FAM- I- LY ____ .
Cmi
E♭/B♭
B♭
E♭
FIN

(12) CLAP YOUR HANDS (Reprise)

(HANDS)
CLAP YOUR HANDS
YEAH!
E.
A/E
E
A/E
FIN

(13) LOOICE (Reprise)

FIN